FOOTBALL

A Crabtree Branches Book

THOMAS KINGSLEY TROUPE

School-to-Home Support for Caregivers and Teachers

This high-interest book is designed to motivate striving students with engaging topics while building fluency, vocabulary, and an interest in reading. Here are a few questions and activities to help the reader build upon his or her comprehension skills.

Before Reading:
- *What do I think this book is about?*
- *What do I know about this topic?*
- *What do I want to learn about this topic?*
- *Why am I reading this book?*

During Reading:
- *I wonder why...*
- *I'm curious to know...*
- *How is this like something I already know?*
- *What have I learned so far?*

After Reading:
- *What was the author trying to teach me?*
- *What are some details?*
- *How did the photographs and captions help me understand more?*
- *Read the book again and look for the vocabulary words.*
- *What questions do I still have?*

Extension Activities:
- *What was your favorite part of the book? Write a paragraph on it.*
- *Draw a picture of your favorite thing you learned from the book.*

TABLE OF CONTENTS

WIDE OPEN!..4
Football History..6
Football Season 8
High School Football Teams 10
Basics of the Game...12
Football Positions: Offense 14
Football Positions: Defense 16
Football Positions: Special Teams 18
Equipment & Uniforms..20
Practice and Training... 22
Football Jargon..24
Playoffs and State Tournaments 26
Conclusion.. 28
Glossary 30
Index 31
Websites to Visit 31
About the Author..32

WIDE OPEN!

The ball is snapped and you sprint downfield, your **cleats** kicking up grass. You cut left. There's not a single defender nearby. You look up and see the football spiraling your way. With a quick jump, you catch the ball. First down!

Throw on your shoulder pads and helmet! We're about to learn why football ranks among the... TOP HIGH SCHOOL SPORTS.

FUN FACT

Football is considered the most popular sport in the United States.

FOOTBALL HISTORY

Compared to other sports, football is pretty new. It was born from two existing sports, **rugby** and soccer. Players from two colleges held the first game in New Brunswick, New Jersey on November 6, 1869.

McGill vs. Harvard, 1874

The game caught on and the rules of play **evolved**. Instead of kicking the ball across the field like soccer, players carried the ball.

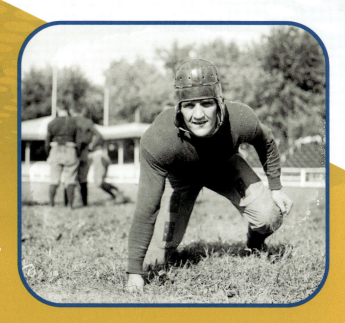

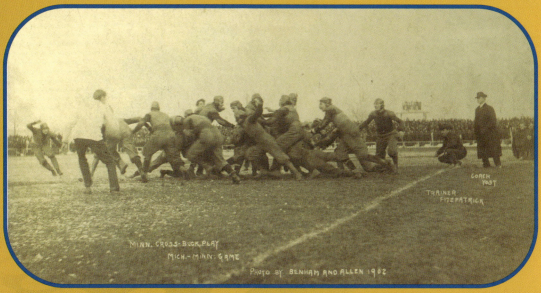

Walter Camp was the man who many refer to as the "Father of American Football." He developed different rules and team positions that changed the game. Camp also introduced quarterbacks, the line of scrimmage, and the scoring system. Because of his love of the sport, the game of football changed for the better!

FOOTBALL SEASON

In many high schools, the football season starts in fall, at the beginning of the school year and is played up until the beginning of winter. There are usually no more than ten games per season, unless the team **qualifies** for the championship.

Football was once a boys only sport, but in the past few years more and more girls are playing too!

FUN FACT

During the 2018-2019 school year, a record 2,404 girls played on high school tackle football teams.

HIGH SCHOOL FOOTBALL TEAMS

High schools usually have at least two football teams, depending on the school size. The varsity team is usually made up of third- and fourth-year students. The school's strongest athletes end up playing at the varsity level.

Junior Varsity

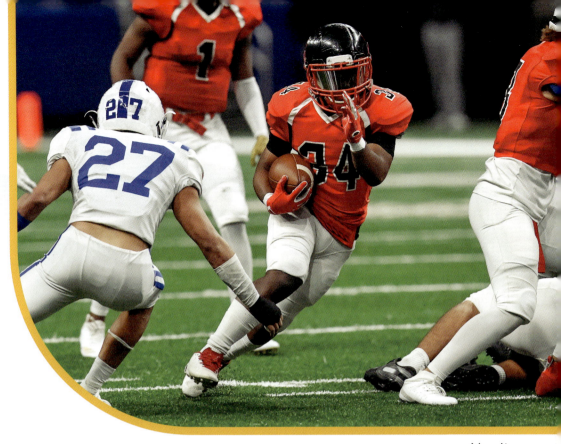

Varsity

Junior varsity teams are often first- and second-year students, giving them a chance to play. Athletes who excel at this level usually move on to the varsity level.

High school football uses the same size football as those used in the National Football League (NFL) games.

11

BASICS OF THE GAME

The concept behind football is simple. Move the football to the end zone to score. The offensive team has four attempts, or "downs" to advance. The defensive team is trying to stop them.

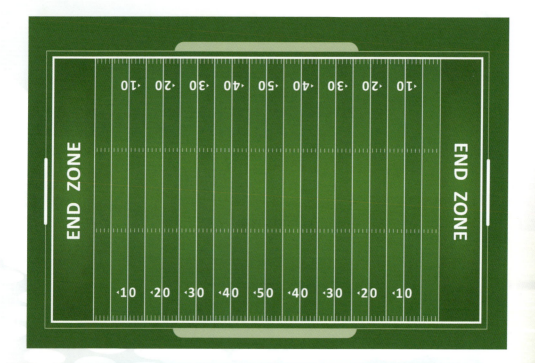

FUN FACT

In Canadian football, the offense is only allowed three downs to advance 10 yards. Football in the United States uses four downs.

Six points are given to the team that gets the ball into the end zone. An extra point is awarded for kicking the ball through the **goal posts**. Referees keep their whistles ready to stop play for penalties they see on the field.

FOOTBALL POSITIONS: OFFENSE

Positions can vary on a football team. Here's a standard lineup for offense:

Center — snaps the ball to the quarterback to begin the play

Offensive Line (4) — two guards and two tackles work as a wall to protect the quarterback

Quarterback — the player who receives and decides what to do with the ball. They can pass, hand it off, or run the ball

Running back — can run the ball up the middle or along the side of the field

Full back — blocks defensive players from tackling the running back

Wide receiver — players who run down field to receive passes from the quarterback

Tight end — a player who blocks on running plays and can receive passes

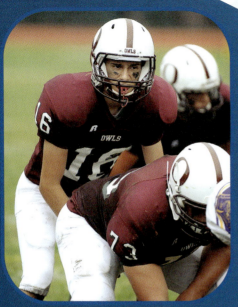

QUARTERBACK

WIDE RECEIVER

CENTER

There are other positions that can be swapped in, depending on what is needed out on the field. One of them is the half back who can run the ball and block. Another is the split end, who can run the ball or divert the focus of defensive players elsewhere. High school football teams like to use split ends to mix things up!

FOOTBALL POSITIONS: DEFENSE

A great **defense** is the key to winning games. Here's the defensive lineup:

Defensive Line (4) — two defensive tackles and two defensive ends who rush toward the quarterback to stop passing plays. They also tackle players running with the ball

Linebacker (3) — their mission is to stop ball runners and catch passes intended for receivers. They can also tackle, or "sack," the quarterback

Cornerback (2) — these two will stay attached to the offensive receivers to make sure they don't catch their passes

Safeties (2) — these players are usually positioned to stop passes and as a safety net for running backs who "got away"

SAFETY

CORNERBACK

LINEBACKER

DEFENSIVE LINE

17

FOOTBALL POSITIONS: SPECIAL TEAMS

Special teams are the players that are on the field during kicks. They are involved in kickoffs, **punts**, field goals, and extra point attempts.

Though they're not on the field as often as the offense or defense, special teams can make or break a football game!

PUNTER

KICKER

If a team's offense isn't able to move the ball close to first down territory by the end of the third play, they may want to punt instead of using their last down. This allows them to kick the ball further down field, forcing the defense to start back further from the end zone.

EQUIPMENT & UNIFORMS

High school football is a rough sport and injury can occur without the proper gear. Helmets protect players' heads and shoulder pads make tackling less painful. Cleats prevent slipping on the grassy field. Players wear mouth guards to keep their teeth and mouth from getting injured.

Football jerseys display the player's number and last name on the back. Pants with pads built in protect the player's legs.

FUN FACT

Dick Plasman was the last NFL player to play football without a helmet. He played without head protection from 1937-1941. When he returned from the military to play in 1943, helmets had become mandatory.

PRACTICE AND TRAINING

Most high schools start football training camps a month or more before school starts. These can be long, tough days designed to push players to their limits. The goal is for the coaches to build a team with their 22 best players.

During the school year, practices are held after school. Coaches will work with players on offensive plays, defensive strategies, and to sharpen skills.

23

FOOTBALL JARGON

Like most sports, football is loaded with strange phrases that might not make sense at first. Here are some to get you started:

Blitz — more than the usual number of defensive players working to confuse and panic the quarterback

End Zone — the ends of the field the offense is trying to reach to score

Hail Mary — a long, desperate pass with little chance someone will catch it

Interception — when the defense catches a ball intended for an offensive player

Line of Scrimmage — the imaginary line where the ball is set for each play. No one can cross the line of scrimmage until the ball is snapped

Sacked — when the quarterback is tackled before he or she can pass or hand the ball off

SACK

LINE OF SCRIMMAGE

PLAYOFFS AND STATE TOURNAMENTS

High school football teams usually compete with other schools to see which team is the best. Schools can participate in state or provincial playoffs and championship **tournaments**.

Teams are broken into classes, based on the total number of students in the high school. This means smaller schools face off against smaller schools. This allows high schools of all sizes to compete fairly!

FUN FACT

Saint Thomas Aquinas High School in Fort Lauderdale, Florida, has won 12 state championships from 1992 to 2020.

CONCLUSION

Football is one of the toughest and most exciting sports high-schoolers participate in. It takes strength, speed, and skill to come out on top. Fans always pack the stands for football games.

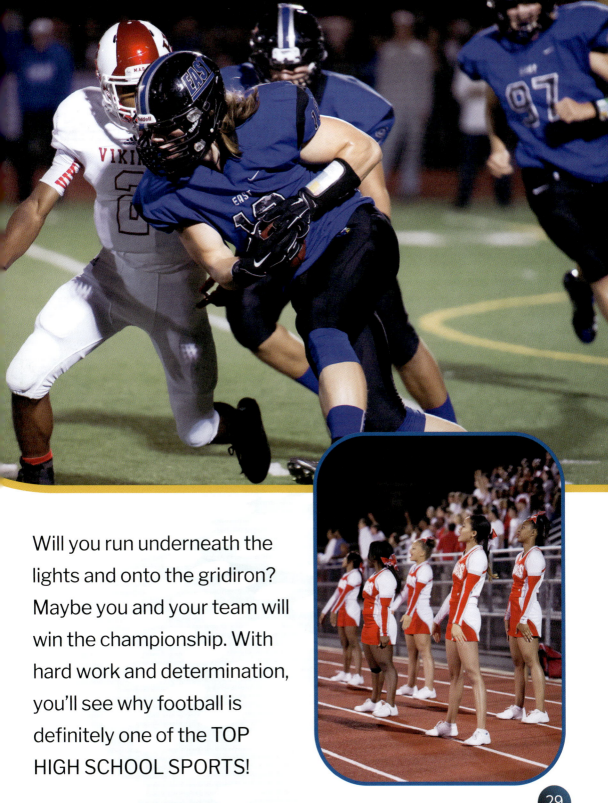

Will you run underneath the lights and onto the gridiron? Maybe you and your team will win the championship. With hard work and determination, you'll see why football is definitely one of the TOP HIGH SCHOOL SPORTS!

GLOSSARY

cleats (KLEETS): special shoes with studs on the bottom to better grip turf or sand

defense (DEE-fenss): defending a goal against the opposing team

evolved (i-VAWLVD): changed a little at a time

goal posts (GOHL POSTS): posts in the end zone that form a "u" shape

mandatory (MAN-duh-tor-ee): required by the rules

offense (AW-fenss): the team possessing the ball in an attempt to score

punts (PUNTS): when a ball is given a handheld kick

qualifies (KWOL-uh-fyes): to meet the requirements of a competition

rugby (RUG-bee): team game played with an oval ball that can be kicked, carried, or passed

tournaments (TOR-nuh-muhntz): a series of contests or games played between competing teams

INDEX

Camp, Walter 7
defense 16, 18, 19, 24
extra point 13, 18
helmet(s) 5, 20, 21
offense 12, 14, 18, 19, 24

quarterback(s) 7, 14, 15, 16, 24
tournament(s) 26, 29
varsity 10, 11

WEBSITES TO VISIT

https://kids.kiddle.co/High_school_football

https://www.gripboost.com/blogs/blog/5-fun-facts-about-your-favorite-sport-football

https://www.dkfindout.com/us/sports/football/

ABOUT THE AUTHOR

Thomas Kingsley Troupe

Thomas Kingsley Troupe is the author of a big ol' pile of books for kids. He's written about everything from ghosts to Bigfoot to third grade werewolves. He even wrote a book about dirt. When he's not writing or reading, he gets plenty of exercise and remembers sacking quarterbacks while on his high school football team. Thomas lives in Woodbury, Minnesota with his two sons.

Written by: Thomas Kingsley Troupe
Designed by: Jennifer Dydyk
Edited by: Kelli Hicks
Proofreader: Ellen Rodger

Photographs: Cover images from Shutterstock.com—background pattern (and pattern throughout book © HNK, football on cover and title page © Billion Photos, cover photos of players © JoeSAPhotos. Also from Shutterstock.com: Page 8 © Larry St. Pierre, Page 9 © Poznyakov, Page 10 © Jim Lopes, Page 11 both photos © JoeSAPhotos, Page 12 © Alesandro14, Page 15 bottom photo, Page 17 top photo © JoeSAPhotos. Following images from Dreamstime.com: Page 4 inset photo © Molly Williams, Page 6 football © Gualtiero Boffi, Page 13 top photo © Sports Images, bottom photo © Danny Hooks, Page 15 both top photos © Sports Images, Page 17 cornerback © James Boardman, line backer © Paul Topp, defensive line © Sports Images, Page 18 © Michael Turner, Page 19 © Sports Images, Page 20 and 21 © Molly Williams, Page 23 top photo © Joe Sohm, bottom photo © Noriko Cooper, Page 24 © Sports Images, Page 25 top photo © Yobro10, Page 27 Stefan Dahl, Page 28 © Molly Williams, Page 29 both photos © Robert Philip. Following images from istock by Getty Images: Pages 4-5 background image © Kalawin, Page 5 football © Gizelka, Page 22 © Manuel-F-O, Page 25 bottom photo © archideaphoto. Page 7 top photo courtesy of the Library of Congress

Library and Archives Canada Cataloguing in Publication
CIP available at Library and Archives Canada

Library of Congress Cataloging-in-Publication Data
CIP available at Library of Congress

Crabtree Publishing Company
www.crabtreebooks.com 1-800-387-7650

Printed in the U.S.A./CG20210915/012022

Copyright © 2022 **CRABTREE PUBLISHING COMPANY**

All rights reserved. No part of this publication may be reproduced, stored in a retrieval system or be transmitted in any form or by any means, electronic, mechanical, photocopying, recording, or otherwise, without the prior written permission of Crabtree Publishing Company. In Canada: We acknowledge the financial support of the Government of Canada through the Canada Book Fund for our publishing activities.

Published in the United States
Crabtree Publishing
347 Fifth Avenue, Suite 1402-145
New York, NY, 10016

Published in Canada
Crabtree Publishing
616 Welland Ave.
St. Catharines, Ontario L2M 5V6